DARK TITAN
NOIR

MASSACRE IN THE DUSK

WORKS BY TY'RON W. C. ROBINSON II

BOOKS/SHORT STORIES

DARK TITAN UNIVERSE SAGA

MAIN SERIES
Dark Titan Knights
The Resistance Protocol
Tales of the Scattered
Tales of the Numinous
Day of Octagon
Crossbreed
Heaven's Called
The Oranos Imperative

Forthcoming
Underworld
Magicks and Mysticism
The Resistance vs. The Enforcement Order

COLLECTIONS
Dark Titan Omnibus: Volume 1
Dark Titan Omnibus: Volume 2
Dark Titan One-Shot Collection

SPIN-OFFS
In A Glass of Dawn: The Casebook of Travis Vail
Maveth: Bloodsport
The Curse of The Mutant-Thing

Forthcoming
Trail of Vengeance
War of The Thunder Gods
Maveth vs. The Swordman

ONE-SHOTS
Maveth, The Death-Bringer
Mystery of The Mutant-Thing
Shade & Switchblade
Retribution of Cain
The Mythologists
Ambush Bot
Kang-Zhu
Cheeseburger Man

THE HAUNTED CITY SAGA
The Legendary Warslinger: The Haunted City I
Battle of Astolat: A Haunted City Prequel (KOBO Exclusive)
Redemption of the Lost: The Haunted City II
Consequences of the Suffering: The Haunted City III (Forthcoming)

SYMBOLUM VENATORES
Symbolum Venatores: The Gabriel Kane Collection
Hod: A Symbolum Venatores Book
Symbolum Venatores: War of The Two Kingdoms
Symbolum Venatores: Elrad's Chronicles
Symbolum Venatores: Mystery of the Magician (Forthcoming)
Symbolum Venatores: Twilight of the Gods (Forthcoming)

EVERWAR UNIVERSE
EverWar Universe: Knights & Lords
EverWar Universe: The Damned Ones (Forthcoming)

PRODIGIOUS WORLDS
Mark Porter of Argoron
Raiders of Vanok
Praxus of Lithonia (Forthcoming)

FRIGHTENED! SERIES
Frightened!: The Beginning
Frightened!: The Light Sky (Forthcoming)

INSTINCTS SERIES
Lost in Shadows: Remastered
Instincts: Point Hope (Forthcoming)
Shadow in the Mirror: Instincts II (Forthcoming)

DARK TITAN'S THE DEAD DAYS
Accounts of The Dead Days
Brand New Day: The Dead Days I (Forthcoming)

OTHER BOOKS
The Book of The Elect
The Extended Age Omnibus
The Horde
The Eleventh Hour: A Chevah Mythos Story
The Supreme Pursuer: Darkness of the Hunt
Massacre in the Dusk

THE DARK TITAN AUDIO EXPERIENCE PODCAST
Season 1: Introductions
Season 2: In a Glass of Dawn
Season 2.5: Accounts of The Dead Days
Season 3: Battle For Astolat
Season 4: Hallow Sword: Cursed

MASSACRE IN THE DUSK

TY'RON W. C. ROBINSON II

CONTENTS

CHAPTER ONE

Bodies piled up in the corners, scattered across the pavements of the alleyway. Lights flickered in the distance as several sirens echoed closer to the alley. Up ahead several police vehicles arrive as the officers move through the alley toward the bodies. They stop in their place, with their guns in hand overlooking the bodies. One of the officers cover their faces to avoid the stench. From there, the coroners were called as they carried the bodies away. The police search the area for any witnesses, only to discover a few homeless people sitting at the edge of the alley. An officer gazed toward them and went to approach. Three of the homeless ran away. Only one had remained, keeping his calm.

"Sir, did you see anything?"

"I saw the blood spill. That I did. I heard the screams. Screams like a banshee. They were echoed in blood. So much blood."

The officer escorted the homeless man to the others as they monitored the coroners. The following day, the news spoke out concerning the murders, calling it a massacre in the dusk. Therefore a manhunt was sent out searching for any suspects which may be related to the victims. While the officers went and searched, they called in a Private Investigator to dive deeper into the murders. An investigator named Luke Cline. Entering the police station was a woman, dressed in casual wear as she began asking for the Commissioner. One officer approached her, seeing her attire and hearing her words.

"You must be the Attorney?"

"I am. I need to speak with the Chief. It's regards this murder case."

"Right this way."

The Attorney went with the officer into the Chief's office. Once she entered, the Chief saw her as he asked for her to sit down. The Attorney reached into her bag, taking out a file and sliding it across the desk.

"You already know why I'm here."

"I do. You have some work concerning this new murder case we're dealing with."

"And I know you called the Investigator. Luke Cline."

"His credentials proved right for this case. He's done these before and has come out with great results."

"I don't think you or anyone in this city understand how Cline does his job. It's not so subtle as one would believe."

"You worked with him before?"

"No. I've studied him. Studied his methods to come the conclusion he is not the one to be called."

"His methods? What about them concerns you?"

"He doesn't follow the strict policies we've laid down. Cline loves to do things on his own term. Granted, he may come in and agree to this case. But, the way he will treat the law is not something one would imply. He's a horror in waiting."

"I see. So, tell me, Attorney Joyce, what would you have me do in this situation?"

"Call Cline and tell him he's no longer necessary for this case. Tell him you have someone else on the job."

"That someone being you?"

"Who else?"

"Ma'am, you're an Attorney. Not a detective. Much less a cop."

She laughed at his words, shaking her head as he slid back the file. Putting it back into her bag, she sighed and gazed around the Chief's office. Her lips smacked.

"You know, I've dealt with a lot of cops in my time. But, there's something different about the ones who operate here. Tell me, what other things have happened since? Before the murders?"

The Chief paused himself, raising up in his seat.

"What are you implying?"

"I'm only asking the serious questions. As an attorney surely would."

"You think you can just plant something on this department? On the officers who do their best here?"

"I don't plant anything. I seek and I find. It's why I'm good at my job."

"Threats don't go well, ma'am. Definitely not in Detroit."

"I'm not threatening you and any officer here. I'm only speaking facts. My truth is this, when I seek out something, I discover it, and I showcase it. A threat is no more than a symbol of one's failure."

"Listen here, you can make up all the threats you want. All the claims you can conjure up in that head of yours. But, I'll tell you this one thing. Cline stays on this case. Whether or not you agree with his motives."

She stared at the Chief and he stared back. Neither one moved from their seats until a knock at the door. The Chief turned his focus, seeing an officer.

"Yes."

"The Investigator is here."

"Tell him to come this way."

The officer went as the Attorney kept her eyes on the Chief. The Chief stood up and walked around the office, looking at photos of his wife and daughter. The Attorney scoffed.

"Sentiment won't be helpful here."

"Who said anything about sentiment?" The Chief asked. "You

have a family?"

"I do not."

"Explains a lot."

Footsteps were heard coming closer to the door as the Chief turned around, seeing Cline standing at the door with the officer. The Chef approached Cline and extended his hand.

"Welcome to Detroit."

The Attorney looked back, seeing Cline shaking the Chief's hand. She was immediacy applauded by Cline's preferred style of dress. Black slacks, black shirt and shoes, with a burgundy leather jacket. Cline entered the office and sat down opposite of the Attorney.

"Investigator Cline, this is District Attorney Maria Joyce." The Chief said. "She is also lending a hand on this case. She suggests she's needed."

"Good to know." Cline replied. "Nice to meet you, Attorney."

She looked at his hand and shook. Her eyes locked onto his. However, to Maria's displeasure, Cline was not a pushover. The tension in his eyes moved her as she pulled back her hand and sighed. Standing up from her seat, she took her leave. The Chief told her they will see each other again before the case is solved. She knew the underline motive. Cline and the Chief both spoke on the details surrounding the case. The sudden massacre, the deceased and the contact of their loved ones.

"Is there anything else I should know about before I begin?" Cline asked.

"Um. Yeah. One of the officers managed to speak with someone in the area near the murders. A homeless man. Said he saw something in the alley before the massacre took place."

"In which alley should I be looking?"

"Midtown District. That's where the alleyway is."

Cline nodded, standing up. He shook the Chief's hand before taking his leave.

CHAPTER TWO

Luke had walked toward the alleyway in the Midtown District. What he saw within seconds were the taped surroundings and the dried blood on the concrete. Walking through the tape, he knelt down and glared toward the blood. So much of it. Not even the water which they sprayed was enough to cleanse the alleyway. Hearing scurrying behind him, Luke arose to find a group of homeless people staring at him. One in particular had a keen eye, scouting the tape and the blood.

"Any of you know what happened here?"

"They don't know a thing." One of the homeless men said.

"What about you? You know anything?"

"I know something."

Luke nodded.

"Then tell me what I need to know."

The homeless man nodded and sent off the others as he walked past the tape and toward the blood-covered grounds. He looked at the walls, seeing stains of splattered blood. Shaking his head. The flickering memories began to flood his mind. Snapping himself out of it to the unusual stare by Luke. He nodded slowly and turned around.

"Didn't realize it was this much."

"What do you know about the massacre?" Luke asked.

"I saw it. First-hand I did."

"You saw it happen?"

"Not the start. But the middle and the end. It was, it was something one dare never to witness."

"Tell me what you saw. Details."

"I saw these people grouping together in the alley. Thought they might've been some teenagers looking to get into trouble. They all came into the alley, ran some of us off."

"The homeless used this alley?"

"Before the killings they did. Not too many and not too often."

"What happened next?"

"Screams and cries echoed across the sky. There was nothing I could do. Any of us. We were powerless in the moment."

"Did you see the killer?" Luke questioned.

"The killer?" The homeless man said. "Um, I'm not sure how to describe it."

"The killer. Was it a man or a woman? Race, hair color. Give me something to go on."

"I would, but I'm not certain as to what exactly killed them. It moved with such speed, only within seconds did they scream and went all silent. Like a pen dropping."

Luke took out a notebook and began writing down everything the homeless man told him and more concerning the alley, the other homeless people, and minor details which relate to the alley. Closing the book, Luke looked down and saw a card smeared in blood. Picking it up, he looked seeing the blood on one side. Flipping I over, the card belonged to a club. He showed the card to the homeless man and his eyes widen and his jaw dropped.

"What's with the look?"

"I know that joint!"

"What is it?"

"It's the nightclub down the block. It's not exactly seen as one from the outside. You know. Due to some certain laws."

"I'm not from this city. So, I have no idea what kind of laws you're referring to."

"Oh, my bad. The club. It's where those youngins' came from. They left the club and came to this alley."

"And you saw all of this?"

"I wouldn't be telling you if I didn't."

Luke nodded, placing the card in his jacket pocket. Walking toward the street, the homeless man followed him. Almost like a beggar without the pleading. Luke stopped, turning back toward the homeless man as he only nodded.

"Why are you following me?"

"Because the club's not open."

"Not open?"

"The club doesn't open till past ten. The area gets pretty crowed around nine-ish."

"So, I'll have to make a return trip tonight."

"Yeah."

"Then that is what I will do."

"Anything else I can help you with? Even though I'll still be in the area."

"You never told me your name." Luke replied. "I'm guessing you have one?"

"Call me Stuggs."

"Stuggs?"

"Yeah. I know it's not a common name. But, names are just names."

"As many say, yet none believe. I'll see you around, Stuggs."

CHAPTER THREE

Once night had come, Luke returned to the District to find it crowded with people. A mixed multitude all standing out in front of the entrance to the nightclub. The women dressed in scandalous apparel. Their faces shrouded with makeup to appease the men entering the club. Luke continued walking as he made his way toward the entrance. Skipping the line without giving any of them a look. The bouncer stepped forward, his hand held up like a wall.

"Where are you going?"

"Inside this establishment. I have questions."

"Well get in in line like the rest of them."

"I'm not here to sow my oats. Move aside or else this won't go well."

"You challenging me, boy?"

"A challenge takes skill. This isn't even a test."

The bouncer moved forward with his hand into a fist. Before making an attack, a second bouncer stepped in. calming his associate and permitting Luke inside the nightclub. Luke grinned as he entered with the first bouncer turning toward the other.

"Why you'd let him in?"

"He's law. No need to make a bigger issue."

Luke stepped into the nightclub, the red hue over his head shrouding the club, feeling the beating of the loud music around him. The odor of alcohol and cigars filled the air. Looking over to his left he saw the strippers dancing before an audience of men. To his right was the bar where several men and women sat down drinking. All their eyes glued onto him as he walked through. Their glares had no effect on Luke. He dusted them off with a smile and a gaze. Stepping toward the bar, he looked at the tender. She looked back at him.

"A guy like you isn't seen in places like this?"

"And how do you know what kind of guy I am?"

"I can tell who's who in this place once they walked through that door."

Luke grinned.

"What can you tell me about this place? Is it this crowed every night?"

"Pretty much. But, tonight is slightly different."

"Different in how?"

"Those men sitting in front of the strippers. they're part of an organization. They come through to collect their shares."

"How do you know of this?"

"I've been here for some time. They talk plainly concerning their affairs."

"Without fear of exposure from the women?"

"Fear is nothing to them but a choice of power."

"Funny how things work. Look here, I'm a Private Investigator. I'm here to speak with the owner of this place. I have questions."

"Questions? What kind of questions?"

"You're aware of the massacre that was discovered down the block?"

"I am. The women here speak about it constantly. Wasn't sure what happened."

"Were any of you outside when it occurred?"

"Some of the women were. They say they heard the screams and ran back inside."

"Can you point me to the women?"

The tender looked up ahead. Her eyes aimed forward with Luke turning around to the strippers. Moving around as they gave the men lap dances with dollars floating in the air. He glanced back at the tender. He was not amused. The tender chuckled.

"You're serious?"

"Yeah. Have to ask them."

"Before I do, one more question. Where were you when the massacre took place?"

"Truth be told. I was in here. Cleaning up the place before my usual clock out."

"I see. Well, best you prepare yourself."

"Prepare for what?"

"Just in case this goes downhill."

Luke stood up from the bar and took a step forward. He stopped, turning back to the tender.

"You never told me your name."

"Why do you want to know?"

"I'm an investigator. Remember."

The tender smiled.

"Madeleine. Madeleine Kay. What's yours?"

"Luke Cline."

"Ah. A strong name. Fits you."

Luke went ahead and stepped down the two-set stairs into the stripper area. Four poles hung from the ceiling as the women danced in front of him. To the men's displeasure, Luke began standing in front of them, nodding toward the women who gave him smiles of pleasure. One of the young men out of the ten stood up, removing his jacket. He tapped Luke on the shoulder.

"What'd you think you're doing?"

"Just getting a nice view."

"Well, get your view somewhere else. You're in our way."

"Oh. Am I?"

"Yeah. Now move."

"I will. Only when I speak with the owner."

A second man sitting down raised his head. He was much older than the first man. Streaks of grey hair covered his face. Staring a hole through Luke.

"The owner? What business you have with him?"

"Law business."

The men stood up from their luxury seats while the strippers moved aside. Nearly all the eyes in the club were on them. Luke held his cool, standing firm as they surrounded him. Each removing their jacket and cracking their knuckles. Luke only grinned while Madeline watched from the bar, taking a drink. The older man stepped forward on Luke.

"Why come in here and start trouble?"

"I haven't started any trouble. From what I see, your buddies are about to start some trouble. I only want to speak with the owner."

"About what? You have a share in this place too?"

"No. About the massacre down the block."

The men held themselves. The older man chuckled while taking a moment to smoke his cigar. The smell of the cigar irritated Luke as he fanned the smoke from his presence.

"Seems this old boy doesn't like the smoke." One of the men joked.

"That's not important." The older man said. "What he's here for is."

"Where is he?" Luke asked.

"He's standing before you, boy." The older man sighed.

Luke's eyes widen as Madeline continued watching. Even the bouncer stood by the door, overlooking the scene while there were others standing outside, banging on the door to have an entry. The owner nodded and told his men to remain at the seats and the strippers to continue their work. He and Luke went and walked toward his office. The music continued as did the strippers. entering the office, Luke sat down as the owner took a stop at his desk. Covering the walls were not posters of women, but landscapes. Mountains, riversides, grassy fields, and deserts. Luke was impressed.

"You taking a gaze ay my wall."

"I am. This place isn't exactly fitting along with the scenery of your club."

"Eh. Well. Not all things are similar in fashion."

The owner laid aside his cigar, taking a seat and measuring Luke's posture. He began to question Luke's reasoning for the visit to Luke's reply was a simple statement of his occupation. The owner was impressed. Having a private investigation inside his club was something he'd never expect. Luke questioned him on the massacre and the owner raised his hands in haste.

"You're not blaming me for the murders, are you?"

"I'm not. I only asked the question."

"Why? Who gave you the idea of coming here and asking?"

Luke reached in his pocket and tossed out the card. The owner saw it and hung his head. Looking at the card, he could see the smeared remains of blood on the opposite end. Throwing the card, he took another moment to enjoy his cigar. Cooling his anger which brew within him. The fact of one of his cards being found at a crime scene struck him. No telling what could've happened if an officer discovered it. His club would've been raided within hours after the bodies were found.

"Where'd you get the card?"

"A homeless guy."

"Homeless?!" The owner yelled. "The fuck did he have one of my cards?!"

"He was near the area when the massacre took place."

"No telling. He's homeless. Of curse he would be out there. Probably heard the screams and all of it."

"Matter of fact, he did."

"See. I was right."

"Said several young people came out of your club and went into the alley. Not sure what they were doing and that is when he heard the screams."

"Young people? Yeah. We get them every so often. You saw the women standing outside before you entered didn't you?"

"I did. Is it like this all the time?"

"Mostly. The club is one of the successful businesses on the District."

"You're sure about that?"

"Damn straight I am. I have the records."

"That's good." Luke said. "By the way, I won't be needing them. No worries."

"Now. That! That is good."

"Your bartender told me several of your strippers were outside when they heard the screams. Said they bolted back inside for safety."

"Bartender? You speak of Madeline?"

"I do."

"Ah. She does her job well. She told you about the strippers?"

"She did."

"Well, I grant you permission to speak with them. And speak only. No touching."

"No worries from me. I'm here on the job."

"Shit please. Those men sitting out there have said the same thing and look where they're at? Getting their laps bounced by strippers."

Luke nodded with a smile. He arose and left the office and went back out into the environment of the club. Something he noticed was the difference of energies from the office to the club environment. They carried two distinctive notices. Luke kept it to mind as he approached the strippers, interrupting their time with the men.

"I need to have a word with each of you."

"The hell you doing?!"

"Step aside, young man." Luke replied. "I have permission from the owner to speak to these women."

"You're interrupting our fun."

"Oh yeah? Then, speak to the owner. He'll tell you all you need to know."

The young man went for an attack, only to be stopped by his colleagues as they walked toward the bar. One of the older men suggested to the younger to grab a drink. He sighed as he stepped away. Luke turned his attention toward the strippers as he sat them down on the luxury seats and he remained standing. The men stared at the bar, watching him converse with the strippers.

"The tender over there told me you ladies were outside when the murder took place."

"She told you that?"

"Would be the new girl." The red-headed stripper said.

"New girl?" Luke asked.

"She started several days ago. Came in out of nowhere. Boss said she impressed him. Guessing she gave him a blow and he hired her."

"So, you're not familiar with her by any means?"

"No. we went out to get some air and while we were talking amount ourselves, we heard the screams coming from down the block. In fear, we ran back inside."

"You didn't see anything? Nothing that may have caught your gaze?"

"Nothing. We weren't even looking in the direction of the screams. Before or after."

Luke nodded as he wrote down their words. The blonde stripper stood up, trying to take a look at the notebook to which Luke closed it and stepped back. Pushing him to see, the blonde began shouting at him while the red-head and brunette attempted to hold her back. The men at the bar heard the shouting and the young one took it as an opportunity. Moving with speed, he attached Luke with several punches. Luke retailed with punches of his own, knocking the young man out. The other men watched and took it as an offense. They all rushed against Luke and attacked him in a circle. Luke did his best to block their blows, even going to the point of fighting back. Hitting a few punches along the way. The owner walked back out to the commotion and called for the bouncers to take Luke out. Grabbing a hold of him as he kicked two of the men in the faces, the bouncers struggled to pull him as he fought back against them. Gaining quick shots to their faces before the men teamed up and forced him outside of the club, throwing him out onto the pavement. Luke slowly stood to his feet and brushed himself. He heard a slight chuckle coming from his left side, turning to have a look, he saw Madeline smoking.

"Guess I missed the brawl."

"Wouldn't exactly call it a brawl."

"So, get what you came for?"

"I did. Thanks for the tip. Could've warned me about the blonde one."

"Funny. I thought all men knew the behavior of women. Particularly the blondes."

Luke smiled with a nod as Madeline took another inhale.

"Seems the trippers aren't fond of you working here."

"And I'm not fond of see them shake their asses and juggle their tits in the company of crooked men. But, here we are."

"Crooked men?"

"You didn't notice their stature? Their demeanor? Their look? Ugh, for a private investigator, you clearly have some things to work on."

"What are you talking about? How are those men crooked?"

"They're mafia." Madeline said, exhaling the smoke.

"Mafia. From what area?"

"That's complicated. Not all of them originate from the same organization. Some are from another one that's based on the east coast. Connecticut, I believe. The others? Probably Dixie Mafia. I'm not certain. You can ask."

"Funny. Like that's going to happen. Especially after what's just took place."

The sky above them cracked with the bolt of lightning. Madeline gazed up to catch the streak as she made her way back toward the door.

"Looks like a storm's coming." Madeline said, dropping the cigarette on the concrete."

"Apparently so."

"Guess you need to take cover. But, not inside of course."

"I wouldn't go back in there anyway."

Madeleine went for the door and stopped. She looked at Luke and nodded with a smile.

"You know, for someone who works in the law industry, you're a decent man."

"Not to sound cliché, but, will I ever see you again?"

"Probably. We'll see." She answered, returning inside the club.

The rain began to pour as Luke returned to his car with the thunder rolling across the city.

CHAPTER FOUR

Luke walked into the police department, seeing Maria standing in the front speaking with the Chief. Hearing the footsteps, she turned around to see him and rolled her eyes. Luke paused himself and glared. The Chief shook his head.

"Don't mind her, Cline."

"I wasn't going to otherwise."

"You will if you want to work on this case." Maria said, facing Luke clearly.

"You're not in charge of this facility." Luke replied. "On what orders should I listen to you?"

Maria looked at Luke's face, seeing the scars. Her eyes widen as she stared at him. Questioning the marks with no words spoken. Luke glared at her before realizing she was referring to the scars. His hand rose as he touched the marks and chuckled.

"What's funny about them?"

"Part of the investigation. That's all."

"What happened yesterday that has your face all scratched up?" The Chief questioned. "Where did you go?"

"To the nightclub close to the crime scene."

"Ah!" Maria jolted. "You figured you would find a good time in the middle of an investigation. Tell me, did the women give you a good dance or were they not capable of treating someone like you with a good time?"

"Enough, Joyce." The Chief said. "Let Cline tell us what

transpired.”

“Before I went to the club, I visited the crime scene. Discovered a homeless man lurking around the block and he informed me of some details. Details which may prove useful in solving this case.”

“I have to guess it was the same homeless man who told one of my officers about the scene. Said he was nearby when it happened.”

“That’s the one.” Luke answered. “His name is Stuggs.”

“Ugh.” Maria said. “What kind of name is Stuggs.”

“At least he has a name.” The Chief responded. “Anyhow, what else did you find?”

“I found a card at the site. I guess the forensics didn’t catch it during their investigation. However, the card came from the nightclub. So, I waited till nightfall and went inside. Spoke with the owner about the murder. A few of his strippers were outside when it happened.”

“And their reaction was?” Maria asked.

“They fled. Ran back inside the club for safety.”

“And the owner of the club,” The Chief said. “What were his words regarding you finding something of his at the site?”

“He requested that he and his club would not become part of the case.”

“But, the card is evidence.” Maria said. “Therefore, the club is part of the case whether he likes it or not.”

“I told him he wouldn’t have to worry about it.”

“Huh. Funny. Making the rules as you go. Just as I’ve been told.”

“Maria, this is not the time ot draw lines between all of us.” The Chief mentioned. “I know you don’t like Cline’s methods. But I don’t give a damn. If he can solve this case, then by all means do what he must do.”

“Whatever.”

The doors of the department opened, grabbing their attention. Luke looked as he saw Stuggs standing, waving his hand in the air while the other officers look to him with a concerned effort. Luke ran in and calmed the officers down before speaking with Stuggs.

"Must be the homeless guy." Maria said. "Figures."

"Why are you here?" Luke asked.

"I have some more information. About the murder. Figured I would tell you."

Luke turned to the Chief with a nod. The two stepped outside the department while Maria looked on with disgust, turning back to talk with the Chief.

"What have you found?"

"The Mafia."

"Mafia?" Luke said. "What about the Mafia?"

"They are involved. Involved in the murders."

"How do you know this?"

"After you left the scene, this black vehicle drove up in front of the alley. Out of it came four men, dressed in nice suits. Wish I could get one."

"Details, Stuggs."

"Oh right! See, these four men went to the back of the car and took out some gas cans. They sprayed the entire alley. Cleaned up the remaining blood and all. Now, the alley looks like it's never been touched. One couldn't tell that a murder took place there."

"Shit!"

"I knew you wouldn't like it. Told you anyway. Just to be on the safe side."

"You have nothing to worry about." Luke nodded. "Now, where did they go after they left?"

"One of them said they were supposed to have some kind of meeting at one of their residences. I don't know where they might be."

"Leave it to me. I'll figure it out."

"Sure thing. Sure thing." Stuggs nodded. "If I come across anything else, I know where to show up."

"That you do."

Stuggs saluted Luke before walking off. Inside the department, Maria and the Chief watched as Luke reentered and approached them. The Chief nodded to Luke, stating to him a well-down. Luke took the complement with only a nod of his own. The Chief returned to his office while Maria stood next to Luke, measuring him.

"I can smell the homelessness all over you."

"You have something to say to me or can we continue on our business?"

"Business is all we have. Besides that, I have something for you."

"Something like what?"

"No worries. I'm not trying to slow you down. I found something that may interest you."

Maria dug into her bag and took out a note. Handing it to Luke, he opened it and saw an address. His eyes turned to Maria in confusion as he waved the note in her face. She didn't like that notion, but took it well. As professional as she could. She placed her hand over the note to stop him from waving.

"What is this?"

"Um, an address."

"An address to where?"

"To a church." Maria answered.

Luke scoffed.

"Why a church?"

"Because the priest of said church apparently knows something about the case. Something major."

"I'm not understanding any of this. How would a priest of a church have information that connects to the case? There's nothing divine about the murders."

"Well, first thing, this church has nothing to do with the divine. Second, the priest requested you by name."

A paused gesture formed on Luke's face. He took another look at the note and inhaled. A small moment to clear his mind even with all the noise of the department around him. Shaking his head, he placed the note in his pocket and told Maria he would head out and visit the church. She only responded with words of clarity. Before Luke left, he asked her what would be her next move. Only with a smack of her lips did she inform him of a witness to the crime and she would be interviewing them. Unimpressed, Luke waved as he left the department.

CHAPTER FIVE

Luke stood outside in front of the church. His eyes were moving left and right as he shook his head. Taking out the note and looking, just to make sure he was at the right place. Luke knew Maria sent him here not only to annoy him, but because she did not want to come and Luke knew why. The church he stood in front of had an upside down pentagram carved on the double doors. Nine steps to reach them and Luke sighed. Walking up the stairs and once he reached the doors, they creaked. Luke nodded. Entering the church, he saw the decorated details of the interior. Red carpet and red pews. Looked as if the entire church was dipped in blood and left to dry in the heat. Perhaps they were according to Luke's own theories he already conjured up. While the doors closed behind him, the air felt uneasy for Luke. The club's atmosphere was a much better condition for Luke to handle than the church's. in front of him, Luke saw a woman, dressed in all black with a dash of red in her hair.

"Welcome."

"Yes. I'm here to speak to the one in charge." Luke replied. "Are they here?'

"Well, our master isn't here."

"Your master?"

"But, the high priest is here."

Luke nodded slowly. Very slowly.

"I'll speak with him, please."

"Very well. I'll go get him."

The woman turned around as Luke called to her. He asked for her name, telling her he was a private investigator. Her eyes grew big as did her smile after hearing his occupation. She nodded and told him her name. Anastasia. She went to the back and after three minutes, the high priest came from the back. Walking past the podium, he looked ahead, seeing Luke standing in the middle of the aisle. He grinned. Luke watched as the high priest approached him and quickly, an eerie sense moved past him through the air. Unable ot make it out, Luke regained himself and focused. The priest stood before Luke, extending his hand.

"You wanted to see me?"

"I do. I hear you're the one in charge."

"I am. Of this place, yes. Why come here?"

"I'm a private investigator. Someone tip me of this place. Apparently there's something you might know about the murders in the alley."

"I heard about them. Shame souls for fall so quickly. Then, why come here?"

"Wanted to ask some questions. See what someone might know."

"I'll shorten your visit. The nightclub down the block from the alley."

"What about it?" Luke asked.

"The answers you seek are there. Sitting inside waiting for you to discover them."

"I've already been to the club. Spoke with the owner."

"You had words with the Don?"

"The Don? No, I talked with the club owner."

"No. no." The priest said. "The club owner you talked to is the front owner. He's only there to stand in the place of the true owner. The Don."

"Explain this to me." Luke said. "Tell me what you know."

"The Don leads much of the mafia business in the District. Therefore, he must keep close hands on all the businesses which surround said District. In every one of them, he's placed someone he can trust to run those operations while he's often away pursuing other ventures. The man you met at the club is one of those men. Put in a position of power by the Don. You want answers? Then ask for the Don."

Luke continued to ask about this unknown Don. However, the answer he kept receiving was to return to the club and ask for him. The priest informed him once he speaks his name, his men will make themselves known. Thereby, brining him to the Don. Luke asked if it might turn into a fight. The priest grinned.

"You know how clubs operate."

"More than you know."

"Oh I know." The priest replied. "I know many things. I've seen your record."

"My record? How do you know about-"

"My people are everywhere, Mr. Cline. In all forms of business. Finance. Law. Medical. Entertainment. Philanthropy. My people keep me informed with all the doings of the world. It's why we stand. Untouched by the outside world."

"You're not like any priest I've encountered. Nor one I've heard of."

"I am unlike many things you're familiar with. Such as it must be for the work at hand. Although I have been labeled a greater kind."

Luke glanced down. Seeing the time. Catching himself, he extended his hand toward the priest. Stating he had to leave. The priest shook his hand and nodded.

"By the way," Luke said. "Mind if I know your name? For the case records."

"Lance." The priest answered.

"First name or last?"

"Last. First name is Vernon."

Luke nodded as he wrote down the priest's name in his small notepad.

"Vernon Lance, huh."

"That is what they call me."

"Vernon Lance. High Priest of the Satanic Temple."

"You got me." Lance smiled. "Anything else I can help you with?"

"No sir. I have what I need. Thanks for the talk."

"Anytime."

Vernon watched Luke exit the temple and once the doors had closed, Lance questioned why Luke would've made his way to him. What brought him to the church and why. Lance believed there was more to the case than he was let on. From there, he turned back and retreated to the back room, returning to his work.

Within the police department, Maria walked to speak with a supposed witness to the murders. The witness had claimed to seen the suspect before the murders occurred. Maria knew she was out of place to interview the witness, such is not within her jurisdiction. Although, she loved to make certain rules for herself. Anything to solve a case. In her mind, her ways are more professional than Cline's. Maria looked at the witness, a young woman who looked as if she was a college student. She somewhat quickened in her seat.

"Relax." Maria said, calming her down. "You're not in trouble."

The young woman understood with a sense of clarity. Taking out a notepad from her bag, Maria sat down, removing the top from her pen as it touched the cream paper.

"Tell me more about the suspect?" Maria asked. "What did

they look like?"

"You won't believe me."

"Trust me, I won't say anything out of the ordinary."

The young woman nodded quickly.

"It was hairy."

"Hairy?"

"All over. Like an animal. Dark fur. I wasn't sure if it was black or brown."

"Yeah. Look, I know it sounds crazy and all, but-"

"You're not lying." Maria nodded. "You're being honest. I can tell."

"I know it wasn't a bear. It walked on two legs."

"Pardon?" Maria paused, putting the pen down. "You mean this thing you saw walked upright? Like a human?"

"Yeah. That's all I know about it. It was hairy and it walked on two legs. I didn't get a good look at it from the front."

"You only caught a glimpse from behind?"

"Yeah. Barely because it was dark and the alley was difficult to see. Only whenever cars would pass by would light enter it."

Maria nodded, writing in the pad and she closed it. Smiling toward the witness. Afterwards, the witness was let go and the Chief visited Maria in the room. He saw something in her eyes. Something pertaining to unawareness. He approached the table, slightly startling her to his amusement, sitting down.

"What's going on?"

"This case is not ordinary."

"What do you mean? the witness said something she wasn't supposed to or?"

"She said the suspect was hairy and walked upright." Maria nodded. "Ever come across something like that? Particularly here in Detroit?"

"Matter of fact, no. We haven't. That's new for us."

"I'm trying to figure out if she saw an animal that looked as if it was walking on two legs. Can't pin-point it."

"What about a bear?"

"She said it wasn't a bear. She was clear on that."

"Then, what other animal could see have saw that night? Only animal I know that could fit the description is a bear. They're able to stand on their hind legs like us and even walk on them. I don't know another animal that could do the same."

"There's monkeys." Maria pointed. "Maybe she saw one of them."

"We don't have wild monkeys roaming around in Detroit." The Chief shook his head.

"Are you certain? Because with the environment, animals can make a change of habit. You know this."

"I do and there is no monkeys in the city. Nor are there gorillas, chimpanzees, or any of those kinds of animals. There's only people and that is that."

Maria leaned in her chair, tapping the pen against the cold steel table. The pen paused.

"Then what did she see that night?"

"Again. I have no idea."

The Chief stood up and approached the door, gazing through the window. He was searching and Maria could tell. She grabbed her notepad, placing it in her bag as she exited the room and the Chief followed her through the moving crowd of officers. The dialing sound of phones echoed as the conversations of the people. The day was indeed a busy one.

"Where are you going now?"

"Back to my residence to do some digging. I want to find out what she meant by this animal. This is becoming very strange. Even for me."

Later in the night, Luke went and took Vernon's words to

mind and returned to the nightclub. Packed as it was the night before. He moved past the crowd of men and women who sought entry. Yells and screams of insults moved over Luke's head as he stood in front of the two bouncers. They glanced at him and remembered.

"Why are you here? Again?"

"I'm here to see someone."

"Like who? One of the women inside or the boss?"

"Maybe both. Right now, it is not the time for delays. This is urgent."

"And what comes of it if we let you in? more fighting like last night?"

"I didn't come to fight. Only to speak with someone inside regarding a case I'm working on."

The bouncers turned to each other and nodded with silence. Their gaze turned on Luke as they moved aside for his entry. Inside, Luke saw the place in the same appearance as the night before, only with some missing chairs and slight shards of broken wood on the floor. He knew where they originated from and walked past them. His eyes went first for the bar and he saw a woman tendering to the drinks. Only, it was not Madeline. Sitting at the bar, the tender approached him.

"What can I get you?"

"Only an answer to a question. Do you know where Madeleine is?"

"Madeleine?"

"She was the bartender last night. I came to see her regarding some business."

"Oh. Well, I've been put here as her replacement."

"Replacement?" Luke jolted. "What do you mean by replacement?"

"She was let go this morning. I don't know why. But, on the bright side, she was not bothered by it. More so relieved."

"And you know this how?"

"Because she told me before she left."

Luke went and asked for a shot of whiskey, in which he drank with speed. Taking a moment of silence, he nodded to himself and thanked the tender for the drink as he made his leave. Stepping outside, Luke found himself surrounded by ten men all dressed in slick suits. Jewelry layered across their hands and wrists. Some wore necklaces of gold and silver. All of which had their eyes shielded with sunglasses. Luke looked around and saw the bouncers entering the club as the customers who waited had moved aside. Luke took a good look at his surroundings. Outnumbered he knew. He balled up his fists and gave the men a grin before tossing the first punch. The nine remaining men all tackled him to the ground and stomped him into the concrete. Luke went and kicked back, trying to stand up only to be kicked in the side and punched in the head.

"This one has spirit!" One of the men chuckled. "Give him another go-around."

The men stepped back as Luke stood. Wiping the blood from his mouth, he extended is hand toward each of them. Calling for another round. The men grinned, cracking their knuckles as they went to attack him. Luke dodged the first round of punches before kneeing one of the other men, shoving him into another. Luke speared one of the men, slamming him to the ground and pummeling his face with his fists. One of the men, much larger in size than Luke grabbed him by his shoulders and tossed him to the sidewalk. Luke caught himself before falling and jumped back up, punching the man while dodging the coming blows from the interfering others. Luke jumped and kicked the man in the face as he fell to the ground. Nine more remained with Luke doing his best to deflect their attacks and give them his own. The customers standing outside began to circle the fight, each of them taking out dollars and betting on the winner. The bouncers exited the club and stood watch. Luke used many methods to take them on. Aside from the casual punches and kicks and knees, Luke went ahead and uppercutted two of the men before backhanding another. He ducked a haymaker from one of the men before snatching him by his collar and slamming him to the ground. Luke took a moment to catch his breath, wiping more blood from his face.

"Who sent you motherfuckers?!"

"Our boss." One of the men answered, showing his fists. "You've trespassed on business which isn't yours."

The man went for a swing, missing the attack as Luke returned it with a punch of his own. Stumbling in his steps, the man paused, holding his nose and seeing the blood. Luke scoffed. Readying himself for another fight. The man jerked his arms and pulled out a gun. Luke stood calm, raising up his own.

"Enough horseplay." said a voice walking in the street.

Luke turned around and saw an older man approaching him. His style of dress was clean. Highly luxurious than the men and their own suits. His tie glistened like a ruby and the jewelry he wore brought him more attention than he realized. Even the customers were in awe of his fashion choices. Luke didn't care. He just wanted to know who this man was and the possibilities of his identities moved through Luke's thoughts. Connections to the club, the men, maybe even the murder. Luke was unsure to know. But, he had a feeling he would be receiving some answers soon and they were standing only a few feet in front of him. The man stood still, his eyes set on the men in suits. He raised his hand and the suited men each took steps back. They stood to attention and cleaned up their suits. Luke was impressed as the man stood before him, looking him up and down. He scoffed with a faint grin. He eyed his men and nodded.

"You have heart, Luke Cline."

"And you know me how?"

"I know everything which transpires in this city. My city."

Luke nodded with a sense of knowing. The man nodded back. They both knew.

"At least I get the opportunity to see you in person." Luke noticed. "Then, you know why I've been coming to your club these past days."

"I do. You seek to find some answers connected to your little case, right? Believing there will be answers inside. So, have you found anything? Anything which can connect the club to said murder? Besides some fancy card, of course."

"The card is evidence. It's proof your club is involved. Those innocent people were inside your club before they were killed."

"And that proves nothing."

"Nothing? That is something."

"A card. Found covered in blood. Blood that made it untraceable for the forensics when they did their petty search."

"How do you know about-"

"Like I said, kid, I know everything that happens in this city. Your actions here are no different."

Luke nodded with anger, shrugging his shoulders.

"So, what now? You take me out and that's it?"

"No. I'm not going to have you killed. You're proven yourself too valuable to be declared dead."

"Then, what are you going to do about me? Even if you could."

The man scoffed with a hint of laughter, pointing at Luke and looking over to his men. The men chuckled while talking amongst themselves about Luke's behavior.

"Well, I'll be go to hell. I'll tell you what, Like Cline. This is my offer. You return to your little case and get it solved. Once you solve it, you leave my city. Is that clear?"

"I'll leave this city once the case is solved. No matter the time needed."

The man sighed.

"With a voice like yours and the attitude, you're lucky I don't have these men tear you to shreds. But, I'm a decent man. A man of character and I've given you my offer. Besides, you have what you came for or did that Satanic priest tell you otherwise?"

"He told me enough. But, I do have one question."

"What kind of question are you pertaining to ask of me?"

"The bartender who was working your club last night. Madeline. Where is she?"

The man nodded with interest. Stepping closer to Luke, placing his hand on his shoulder. Their eyes locked and Luke could see the answer. He needed no words. The man stepped back and extended his hand. Luke looked.

"You know what to do." The man said. "For your best interest, of course."

Luke went and shook the man's hand. He grinned, signaling his men to leave the area. Nearby, a vehicle drove up in front of the club where the door and exited and opened the back door for the man to enter. Luke stepped forward, calling out to the man.

"Yes?" The man asked.

"It was nice to meet a Don." Luke said. "I'm sure the others are like you or somewhat different."

The Don nodded as he entered the car. Luke looked back at the club before taking his leave.

CHAPTER SIX

Luke entered the department the following morning with Maria entering behind him. She tapped him on the shoulder as he turned around. Quickly, Maria saw the bruises and sighed.

"Again?"

"There's no need for your concern."

"I am not concerned. Only questioning your purpose on this case? Does it only revolve around you coming back here with more bruises or what?"

"I ran into some trouble. That's all."

"Trouble? Like the kind of trouble that follows you pr the kind of trouble you cause wherever you go?"

"Doesn't matter. Can we go and talk with the Chief about the case."

"Well, I'll tell you something while we're on our way."

Luke went ahead and walked with Maria keeping up with is pace. She took out her notepad, showing him. He glanced at the pad once and kept his eyes centered.

"I talked with a witness yesterday."

"A witness?"

"Not your little homeless buddy. Someone else who was there the night it happened. They got a look at the suspect. A decent one it seems."

"Tell me. What did they look like?"

"Hairy and walked upright." Maria answered.

"The hell's that supposed to mean?"

"You said you wanted to know. I just told you."

"You said the witness saw the suspect. What you just describe is not a suspect. That's an animal."

"It's what she said."

"Horseshit." Luke replied. "Try again. Find someone else who might know a thing."

Maria shook her head and saw the bruises on Luke's face. Hesitant to ask, he went ahead and the expression on Luke's face could only give the response she didn't seek. Questioning him about the bruises, Luke went ahead and told her everything. From the club to the men and the Don. Maria wanted to rant as she had done before but held in her composure, stating to Luke she will look into the Mafia which Luke encountered. Luke however suggested he would return the favor by visiting them himself and Maria began to warn him about the Don. From his methods and his power over Detroit. Her words began to linger in Luke's mind. How would Maria know so much about the Don, he asked himself.

"You want to say something, don't you?" Maria spoke.

"Just wondering how you know so much about this Don. You encountered him before in some past case?"

"He's been involved in a lot of cases around here and beyond. His real name is unknown to us. Rarely is spotted in the public eye. The fact you saw him last night is a jewel of an encounter. My first encounter was some years ago when there was talking of some kind of "Apprehension" case being discussed across the border."

"The border? A Canadian case?"

"Yeah. I know my jurisdiction doesn't allow me to work on foreign cases. But, I kept my eye on it when I found out the Don had a hand in it. Not sure if he was deeply involved or just had his foot in the door. He's partnered with a lot of powerful people. A network of society some would call it."

"I still would like ot have a word with him. Man-to-man."

"Leave him be. Unless we find something connecting his organization to the murders, there's no need in bothering him. Especially after what you endured last night."

"His organization is involved. The card. It was laying in the alley covered in blood. The victims came from his club that night. As far as I'm concerned, him and his organization are neck-deep in this case. I can't just move aside and let him be."

"You have no choice, Cline." Maria jolted. "No choice."

"On who's authority? The Chief's? or yours?"

"Don't get me started. I was already on the edge after hearing of your hand on this case. Two days later, where has it gotten you? Bruises and cuts across your face and hell, you look like you've barely slept since you arrived."

"My work is necessary. Other things come second."

"Like your health and all?"

"I can take care of myself."

"I'm sure you can. Just don't die before this case is over, alright."

Luke turned around, heading out. Before he exited, he told Maria he would be returning to his residence to do more work on the case. Meanwhile, Maria gave him a final warning pertaining to the Don and his Mafia. Luke took the words in and buried them deep.

While Luke returned to his residence, he began to feel uneasy. Something in the air, maybe? Luke opened the door and for a moment chose to look down. Which he did and what he saw was an envelope. He picked it up and saw only his name written on the front along with the initials, '*MK*' on the upper corner. His eyes squint, thinking of the initials and who they might belong to. Luke didn't know anyone with those initials or so he thought as he sat down and opened the envelope and found a note. Unfolding the shriveled paper, he began to read it.

"What is this?" He asked himself.

The note described an invitation to a masquerade party being held later that night in the district of Metro Detroit. Luke was familiar with the region, having visited there some time ago on a different case. One much easier than the current. At the bottom of the letter, Luke saw the name Madeline and from there he knew. Folding the letter and placing it in his pocket, he grabbed his keys and left the residence.

Luke returned to the department and found Maria having a conversation with the Chief concerning more potential witnesses. Knocking on the door in a frantic state, Luke ran into the office holding the letter in his hand.

"What's gotten into you?" The Chief asked.

"I've found something." Luke answered. "It's connected to the case."

"And what have you found?" Maria asked. "A note of some kind?"

Luke presented the note on the table, laying it next to the three folders with detailed witnesses. Luke didn't mind them as he was clearly focused on the note. It was his key to finding the source of the case. In his mind as the moment. Whereas Maria and the Chief was confused. Their focus was set on interviewing more witnesses who have stated to have seen something that night around the murder area. From neighboring residences to visitors in the district.

"There's a masquerade party being held ot night. In the Metro district."

"Ok." The Chief said. "So, what does a masquerade party have to do with this case?"

"Potentially everything."

"How are you certain of this?" Maria asked. "Did the homeless guy give this letter to you?"

"No. I found it when I returned to my area. It was slid under the door while I was gone."

"Sill could've been your homeless friend."

"It wasn't." Luke said, pointing toward the name at the bottom. "It was her. Madeleine."

"Madeleine?" The Chief uttered.

"Who's Madeleine?" Maria curiously asked.

"She's the woman who put me on the details at the club. She was there when the murders took place and she knew more. But, didn't converse with me to speak more."

"You're saying she knows something about the case and you're just now telling us about her?" Maria pointed with a sheer sense of irritation.

"I didn't know if what she told me was to be true. Until I had my encounter with the Don and his men."

"Don?" the Chief said. "What's been happening around here the past two days?"

"Cline had a fight with the Don's men. The mafia that is well-known in the shadows of the city. The Don let him go. Probably because Luke held himself steady. Proved himself a capable fighter in the eyes of the Don."

"And you know this how?" the Chief asked.

"As I told Luke, I've had encounters of my own with the Don. Past cases and suchlike."

The Chief sighed, his eyes returning to the witness files and the note. He gave a nod as Luke grabbed the note and returned it into his pocket. Maria wanted to say something regarding the note, but kept it within herself. Something she's not very known to do. Luke looked at the witness files and began to ask of them. The Chief told him they were preparing to speak with more witnesses as to what they saw that night. Luke figured they could be useful, but the party would hold more details to the case. The Chief took his words well and understood them. He couldn't force Luke to remain a the department and speak with the witnesses.

"What time is the party?" Maria asked.

"Why do you want to know?" Cline responded. "You're coming along or something?"

"I am. It's a party and you won't be able to learn everything on your own. You do your thing and I'll do mine."

Luke gave a nod. Maria smiled as Luke left the department.

Within the hour, Maria and the Chief began interviewing the witnesses while Luke traveled throughout the city, searching for a mask to where. He already had a suit in his residence. He brings one wherever he goes in case of a need. The party itself is a need. The witnesses began describing an animal. Just as the first one did.

Some said it walked on all fours, comparing it to a bear or a cougar. Others said it walked upright like a human, but its behavior was animalistic. The Chief had hoped one of the witnesses would describe something like a human being, but neither of them did. All were details of a animal that killed the people in the alley that night.

Once the witnesses' interviews were over, Maria took her leave and prepped herself for the party which was being advertised across the city for those who would attend. At his residence, Luke dressed himself in a suit. In his mind, he felt off. His usual clothing fits his personality more than a nice suit. He felt fake within his soul. He had a mask sitting in the car as he headed out.

CHAPTER EIGHT

Stepping into the party, Luke saw himself surrounded by dozens of people. All of them had their faces covered with masks ranging from Halloween-esque figures to the renaissance era. Luke's mask was only a simple doll-like mask, only in black. Walking into the party behind him was Maria, who stood out from among the people with her fiery red Mardi Gras-like mask and dress. The eyes of the many were locked onto her style of fashion. Even Luke gave her a nod.

"You weren't expecting me to show up like this?"

"Figured you would've come here as you were at the department. All business-like."

"Well, we are on business. Just had to blend in. now, where do we start?"

"I figured we should find out who's here exactly. That way we can actually point out whatever it is that we should know."

"Good. I'll take the area over on the left."

"Why?"

"Because I see several men. Their suits are expensive. I believe they may be working with the Don."

"Then, leave them to me."

"Oh no." Maria laughed. "You already had your time with them. I'll handle it this time. Make it smoother to get across."

"And what should I do? Walk around this party like some kind of creep?"

"If you want. But, there is a bar over there. I'm sure you know what to do."

"I'm aware. Keep me posted on your progress." Luke said, walking off.

"Same to you."

While taking his time to reach the bar, a arm grabbed him and pulled him to the wall opposite of the party. Luke stared at the one responsible. Seeing it was a woman as she removed her plague doctor-like mask. Luke saw her face and removed his mask in response.

"Madeleine."

"Surprised to see me here."

"Hold on. Why are you here?"

"I'm on duty."

"Duty? Luke paused. "What are you talking about?"

"It's a long story and I prefer not to waste any more time."

"You have some explaining to do."

"Like what? How I worked at the club that one night, then vanished out of the blue?"

"Yes. Who are you? Truly."

Madeleine sighed as she grabbed a nearby chair from the table and sat down, facing the crowd with Luke leaning against the wall. Crossing his arms as he waited. Madeleine pointed at him. Seeing his demeanor oozing from him. She could only let out a smile. Luke looked at his chest and back.

"What is it?"

"Nothing. Just, the way you're standing there. All manly. I like it."

"Please, explain yourself." Luke responded slowly.

"Ok. I came into the city a week ago on a secret project. Still I do not know the name of the project, but anyways. My first duty was to learn more about the Don. My boss informed me of his works scattered across the country. Eventually, a trail was made that led his busiest operations being held here in Detroit. So, as my first progress, I obtained a job at his club. A bartender. Figured it would be easy. Sure worked on you didn't it?"

"Keep going."

"So, after our meeting at the club and your little tango with those men, I saw the Don entering the club. He went to have a chat with the owner. The man you spoke to that night."

"I see. What else?"

"I was charged with providing them the drinks for their secret meeting. I heard everything I needed to and the next day, I chose to quit. Said the air of the club was too much for a little girl like me."

"And that leads you here? How did you know I would be here?"

"Because I'm the one who left you the note."

"The note was from you?"

"Of course. With the help of Stuggs, too."

'Stuggs knew about this?"

"Yeah. How else was I to find out where you stayed. Stuggs keeps a clear eye on your place. Just in case someone who's not friendly decides to make a move. He may be homeless, but he's got heart. A good one at best."

Luke nodded. Taking a small peek back into the party. His eyes moved through the people in search of Maria. Madeleine noticed it as she glanced out into the field of people.

"So, who's the woman you tagged along with for the night? Some other one you found on your way here?"

"No. she's a district attorney. Working on the same case as me."

"An attorney. That's well to know. I'm guessing she doesn't know about me, does she?"

"Not exactly."

"Perhaps, I should introduce myself to her. See how this all works out.”

“No need. Maria and I have everything under control.”

“You do? So, have you discovered what the Don has been working on?”

“We have not. That is why Maria is having a conversation with his men.” Luke said, pointing.

“Oh. Those aren’t his men.” Madeleine noticed.

“What do you mean?”

“Well, they are his men. Low ones I mean.”

“Then, where are the ones we need to speak with?” Luke asked with a hint of hastiness in his voice.

“You don’t find them. They find you.”

Taking another look toward Maria, they see three men approach her. She turned around without a notice as two of them grabbed her by her arms and took her elsewhere in the building. Luke went to help, only for Madeleine to hold him back.

“What are you doing?”

“Relax, they aren’t going to kill her.”

“How would you know?”

“That’s not how the Don operates. Right now, what we should do is follow them. Quietly.”

“And let them lead us to the Don.”

“Yes. You’re learning. For a private investigator, you still have some kinks to work out.”

“Another time. Let’s get moving. They’re taking her upstairs.”

“Figured he would be up there. Probably staring out of the window like some kind of boss. You know they do that.”

Moving through the crowd, their eyes remained on the staircase, seeing Maria being marched upward. She looked out into the crowd and saw Luke staring at her with Madeleine by his side. Her eyes told him a directive. He nodded. Turning to Madeleine to speak, however, she knew what Maria had informed him. To his surprise, Madeleine went ahead toward the stairs with

Luke following. Walking up the stars, Luke saw Maria being placed inside a room and sitting at the desk near the window was the Don.

"He's there." Luke said. "In the office."

"As I figured. So, how do we get in there?"

"We wait and listen. See what he tells her. Once, we have enough information, we'll make our mark."

"Understood. But, what about those two?" Madeleine pointed, seeing two guards standing near the double-doors.

Luke looked at them. He measured with his eyes and saw on their right sides a firearm. Nodding his head, he began instructing Madeleine of his plan .she agreed to the plan and quickly made her move. Taking off one of her shoes, she tossed it near them, startling them.

"What was that?" One had asked.

"I don't know. Check it out."

One of the men went and checked to see the cause of the noise. Walking further from the door, Luke went up and choked out the second man while Madeleine went and hit the first man in the head with her other shoe. His body flopped to the floor, causing a small sounding thud. Luke looked up toward her as he was pulling the first man from the door to the wall. Sitting him down as he appeared to be sleeping. Taking his gun for same measures, he told Madeleine to do the same. Grabbing the gun last after she placed her shoes on.

"What's next?" Madeleine asked. "We go in?"

"No. we listen."

"Listen? You're sure we'll be able to hear what they're saying in there?"

"Hush."

"Yes sir." She smiled.

Taking the moment to hear, inside the office, the Don sat at the desk staring at Maria, who was surrounded by the two men who brought her to the room. Maria was not afraid, nor was she concerned. The Don knew it and he wasn't bothered. Familiar with one another. They talked like old colleagues, only with Maria bringing several of his past crimes. He laughed them off while taking a drink of vodka from his glass.

"You're still bummed out about those incidents? Maria, when will you ever grow up and look to the stars."

"I've looked well enough. What you're doing will come out to the public. They always do."

"Not if you own the press."

"Some things have a habit of slipping out."

"And when they do, we will cover them up with an opposite story. A story much more vigorous than the other. The media here is under our control. What the masses see is what we want them to see. The real world, hmm, if they knew what was happening. The truth of the matter, they would revolt. But, such responses to our work, we cannot tolerate it."

"You know what's going on about he case, don't you." Maria asked. "You know who killed those people in the alley."

The Don grinned, standing up from his seat and looking out toward the city.

"Maria, you've encountered all types of criminals in your line of work, correct?"

"I have."

"But, you've never had the chance of seeing a culprit that's beyond human means. Beyond human understanding."

"What are you getting at?"

"I know who killed those young people in the alley that night. I know what it caused. That is why my work is silent on this matter. Why my men have been occupying the club ever since and before."

"What aren't you telling me? Who killed those people? Who is the murderer?"

"Before I speak of this any further, what did those witnesses tell you?"

"How do you know about the witnesses?"

"Like I said. I have eyes everywhere. Even in that department you believe is covered by some form of justice."

"You have some on the inside?"

"I have someone everywhere. This city is under my control. Again, Maria, you know how all of this works. You don't have to be he mayor of a city to control a city's progress. All it takes is money. That money will form a network of very powerful people. Giving one access to much more than they could imagine. Such a network with that kind of money begets power and, you know the rest."

"Just let it out."

"I'm sorry. Let what out?"

"The murderer. Tell me who is it so I can bring them in and close this case."

"It's not so simple. The murderer is not someone you can easily track down and find."

"Give me a name."

"A name." The Don laughed. "And what will you do with a name? trace it in your data mines? Oh no, this culprit you call it, is again, not someone you can easily find."

"Give me a fucking name!" Maria yelled.

"Keep that tone silent before I force it to remain quiet."

"My hands aren't tied. Neither are my feet. Don't make me do something you'll regret, Marquis."

"Using my first name, huh? In front of my men. Such actions are not permitted, Maria. Therefore, I must make an example."

The Don reached into the desk drawer, taking out a pistol and a silencer. Maria jolted from her seat as the two men held her down. She struggled to get free as the Don prepared the firearm. Twisting the silencer. He grinned. Walking over to ward her and leaning against the desk. He held the gun toward her forehead. Maria grunted as he head tapped the muzzle.

"You bright this upon yourself, Maria. Now, what will the people do when they never learn the cause of the massacre."

The door bolted open with Luke and Madeleine standing. Maria looked back, seeing them. She regained control of her arms and elbowed one of the men in his nether regions before knocking the gun from the Don's hand. The other guard pulled out his firearm, only to be shot by Luke. The gunshot had reached the bottom floor and the people began evacuating. Maria jumped from the chair and ran toward Luke and Madeleine as the Don retried his gun and fired back. The three ran back t the floor, being scattered with the people.

"Get yourselves out of here!" Maria yelled. "I'll meet with you later."

"Where are you going? Luke asked.

"To find some answers."

Making their way outside, the two saw Stuggs waiting for them.

"Just in time." Madeleine said.

"What are you doing here?" Luke asked.

"The woman told me to come just in case of a disturbance. I see there was one after all."

"We need to get out of here." Luke said toward Madeleine.

"Not yet."

"Why not?"

"Because, you see that tunnel there? We need to get in there now."

"Why would we do that?" Luke wondered.

"It's where the Don keeps his research and documents." Stuggs answered.

"How are you aware of this?"

"I spend my time going around the city. I learn things."

"If we can get in there, won't we need a key?"

Madeleine turned around after digging in her dress. She raised up a key to Luke's amusement. Stuggs giggled as they moved toward the tunnel. Several of the Don's men stepped out and searched the grounds, only to see the people running in fear for their lives. Others just stood outside huddling with others.

CHAPTER NINE

Inside the tunnel, Luke looked around. The walls were made of brick. Looked like something from the early 1930s to the 1940s. The stench of alcohol was within the air. Like it might've been soaked into the walls. Stuggs took a sniff and savored it. Madeleine moved through the tunnel, noticing the darkness within growing. Madeleine began wishing she had a torch. Stuggs suggested he go back out and make one with some junk he could find. Luke silenced them and stepped forward, taking out a flashlight from his suit. Madeleine smirked.

"You always carry one with you?"

"I come prepared. No matter the circumstance."

"That's good." Stuggs replied. "Very good. I do the same, you know. With what I have. At best."

"This place must've been used during the prohibition period." Luke noticed.

"You're right about that." Madeleine responded. "That is why the Don chose it as his secret place. Most of the people have forgotten about hidden caverns and likewise."

Continuing their walk for almost another three minutes, they reached a door. Upon the steel structure was an insignia. Something of a triangle mixed with a hexagon. The symbol was unfamiliar to the three of them. Stuggs shrugged his shoulders.

"Is it supposed to be a new shape or something?"

"No." Luke answered. "This is something else. Something not to play around with."

"You're familiar with these kinds of symbols?" Madeleine asked.

"I've had my share of encounters. Being a private investigator brings you into contact with all types of people and the things they believe in."

Taking a closer look at the insignia, Luke noticed the letter 'W' carved into the hexagon, scratching through the triangle. Madeleine placed her hand upon it, her fingers rubbing against the rugged symbol. To her surprise, the insignia was made of a different material than the door. With the door being made of steel, the symbol was made from something else. Something perhaps more durable than steel. However, they did into bother with what mineral was used and she used the key to unlock the door. The door creaked as they stepped forward. Luke had used the flashlight to find a switch and he did, only a few feet from the door against a podium. The light brightened and what they saw in the room gave them a slight startle. Stuggs was amazed at what he saw. Running over to one of the tables, seeing swords and daggers.

"You see all of this?!" Stuggs yelled. "Who knew the mafia was into some medieval shit."

"You see all of this too?" Madeleine asked Luke.

"Yeah. I do."

Luke looked all over the room. Swords, axes, and spears hung against the walls. Paintings of ravaging animals layered across the other wall from wolves, bears, mountain lions, and lynxes. The third wall had a map of the city and the markings upon it had matched previous cases. The smell of alcohol still lingered within the room, yet there was another stench that covered itself under the smell. Luke knew the second stench. Madeleine asked only for Luke to confirm his suspicion.

"Blood."

Taking a closer look toward the map and the markings listen upon it. Luke's understanding, several murders occurred in those marked places. Still staring at the map, Madeleine pointed. One red mark was placed on the alleyway near the club.

"He knew."

From the doorway arrived several of the Don's men. With them were three scientists. The scientists screamed as the shootout took place. Stuggs ducked into a corner while Luke and Madeleine shot fire against the Don's men. Taking several of them out. The remaining ones bolted into the room and returned fire. Stuggs looked out, seeing the men shooting toward Luke and Madeleine. Sitting close to the table, Stuggs raised his head and saw a knife sitting. He grabbed it and with his best effort threw the knife toward the shooter. To his surprise, the knife made its mark, stabbed into the shooter's ankle. Screaming in pain, Luke came from behind the podium and fired the shot. The scientists stood with fear as Luke approached them.

"We're not one of them!"

"Then who are you?!"

"We're scientists! We work with the Don on several projects."

"Why would the Don need scientists to work on his little things?" Madeleine questioned. "What are you helping him with?"

"He didn't have the resources to achieve what he desired." The second scientist said. "So, he contacted us for assistance and with our combined efforts, we achieved what he sought."

"And what did he seek out?" Luke asked.

"Lycanthropy."

"Huh?" Stuggs said, bolting up from the corner.

"He began wondering how he could increase the power of his mafia. Preferably the men who keep his operations protected. He told us having simple humans wasn't enough and he wanted more. Something much more refined for protection. First thing was super soldiers, but they proved unsuccessful. Then the idea of hybridization came into discussions. The Don believed we needed an alpha animal to merge with a human host in order to complete his desired ideas. We tried many operations with a few of his men. Those who trusted him till death. Many died in the trials."

"Yet." The second scientist said. "Only one managed to survive."

"And what happened to one who lived?" Luke asked. "Is he still around? Doing the Don's bidding?"

"He's still around. But, he's not like us anymore."

"He's stronger now." The first scientist said. "Much stronger."

"It makes sense now. Everything he was saying in the office. Everything he told Maria." Luke said. "The Don's been working on something here in secret. Something very-"

"Horrifying." Stuggs said, looking inside a book.

"What are you holding?" Luke asked, looking over toward Stuggs.

"This book. It was laying right here. It was already open."

They went and looked at the book. The pages within were detailed with old writings. Estimating the age of the writings, Luke believed them ot have been written sometime in the late 1800s. Madeleine 's estimate was around the mid-1910s. But, what was drawn on the pages began to cause a stir within them. The drawings were illustrations of a beast. A hairy beast. Sharp fangs and claws. Its red eyes were even detailed to the point, they could be its own eyes engraved on the page.

"Is that a werewolf?" Madeleine questioned.

"I'm afraid it is." Luke answered. "No. this can't be real."

"Then, what do you explain of this? The book? The weapons all over the walls? The smell of blood being covered up by whiskey. Believe it or not, I think we've found the culprit of the massacre."

"I'm sorry to inform you, it's very real." The scientist replied.

"I thought the smell was of gin." Stuggs said. "Guess I was wrong."

Luke took out his phone to dial Maria. Although, the signal was low due to being in the tunnel. Moving with speed. He asked them did they catch a glimpse of the moon before they came into the room. Madeleine said no. Stuggs gave a nod to the question.

"What did it look like?"

"Like it always does."

"No, Stuggs." Madeleine said. "He means how did it look? Crescent, full, new?"

"Oh. It was full. "The second scientist spoke. "You didn't realize how bright it was out there?"

"That wasn't my concern." Luke replied. "Yet, now it seems we have to deal with this now before another killing is committed."

Making his leave, Luke grabbed the book and took it for evidence.

"I'm not sure you can take that, sir." The scientists both said.

Luke turned back with the gun facing them. The scientists paused themselves and startled in their shoes. Both raised their hands in fear. Luke questioned them about the operations and they said their work was finished. Luke waved the gun, allowing the scientists to escape. They ran out of the room like rats. There was no slowing down. Madeleine watched them as they ran and tripped in the darkness of the tunnel.

"You're sure about letting them go?"

"No worries. They'll expose themselves once this is all over. Their hands are all over the operation here."

Madeleine had locked the door in case one of the Don's men would return. Making their way back to the outside, Luke glared up to the clear sky and he saw the moon. In full and shining bright. Madeleine began questioning their next move. Luke responded by informing Maria of the news. He called her.

"Maria, listen, we've found something regarding the case!"
"Get to the alley now!" Maria screamed. "It's here!"
"What's there?!"
"Get here now!"
The call ended with Luke looking around.
"What is it?" Madeleine asked.
"It's out."

CHAPTER TEN

Riding through the streets in Luke's vehicle, they managed to arrive nearby the crime scene with Maria ducked down behind one of the vehicles. The three came to her aid and saw the terror in her eyes. She pointed over to the alley where the bodies were found and Luke was determined.

"What are you doing?" Madeleine asked.

"I'm going to see if this thing is true."

"You already know the answer."

"Make sure you guys are safe. This has to end."

Luke moved with as much quietness he could muster. Reaching clover to the alley, he saw what he knew he would see. A living werewolf. Standing at nearly seven feet in height. The claws shined with the light around the streets and its howling breath gurgled through the air. The wolf knelt and sniffed the concrete. Sensing the blood, it began licking the ground. Luke raised up from behind the vehicle and fired a shot. The wolf jumped, its head turning back and the eyes glaring toward Luke.

"Shit." Luke said. "It's real."

The wolf let out a roar as it ran toward Luke. He fired another shot, the bullets went through the wolf's shoulder. The wolf stumbled. Blood poured from the wound. Luke continued firing more shots, slowing down the beast. The wolf came closer and swiped its claws, tearing down the car Luke stood behind. He moved toward the next one as the wolf continued to destroy the cars with only its claws. The wolf's veins glowed a bright green. Luke had seen something similar in the tunnel. A tube connected to a machine. There was a form of liquid in the tube. A green liquid. Connecting the dots, Luke knew the green material was the power source between the wolf and the man. Luke fired a shot into the veins as the green liquid oozed from the wolf's arm.

"I have you now." Luke said.

The wolf shook off the pain and lunged in the air toward Luke. Taking one aim, Luke fired the shot and the bullet made its mark. Hitting the wolf in the head, causing the body to collapse to the ground. The wolf was now declared dead and Luke stood over it, making sure the creature was truly dead. Unaware as to how the gunshot could've killed the wolf. Maria, Madeleine, and Stuggs approached him. Questioning how one shout could've killed the creature. Maria told him silver bullets were capable of killing werewolves. Luke had checked the rounds of the gun, seeing all the bullets were silver.

"A fail safe?" Luke questioned.

"Probably in case one of his experiments had turned on him. He must've equipped all his men with silver bullets."

"So," Stuggs said. "What's next?"

"We find the Don and bring him in." Maria answered.

The following morning, the police all came out and discovered the Don's men inside the club. They were all arrested, even the owner of the club was taken. The search for the Don continued for several days, only for Maria to discover he made a trip to Europe. Knowing her jurisdiction, she couldn't go after him. She made a phone call to a friend and informed them of the details. A day later, the Don was caught and brought back to the States. The case was officially solved. Yet, the exposing of a werewolf remained a secret between all parties. Luke prepared himself to leave Detroit with Madeleine agreeing to accompany him. Maria had found him outside his residence while Madeleine jumped into the vehicle.

"I see she's going with you to wherever you're off to."

"The case is solved. My time is done here."

"I understand. However, if there is another case to be solved here, perhaps they can call you again."

"It seems you've warmed up to me." Luke grinned.

"For the moment. You proved useful for this case. That's something I can respect."

"I can get behind that."

Luke entered the car as Maria walked toward the door.

"So, what's next for Private Investigator Luke Cline?"

"I'm not certain. I thought this world was only dealing with criminals and drug lords. Now, with this new revelation of werewolves, there must be more out there to discover. To learn. So, that's where I'll be heading."

"To find more werewolves?"

"To learn more about the world." Like nodded. "We have no idea as to what truly dwells among us."

Maria nodded, stepping back from the car. giving her farewell to Luke and his to her. Luke and Madeleine rode off out of Detroit, where a new discovery may very well be set.

1

New Haven Detective and U.S. Marshal Preston Maddox drives down a pair of narrow streets as he's on the search for Jonny Cartel, one of the top drug lords of New Haven, Connecticut. Preston, who's wearing his casual suit attire, drives through the quiet streets of New Haven. He turns a corner that heads toward Orange Avenue, around the West River.

"I take it he's around this area. Somewhere."

He turned a corner, which was leading him into a dark pathway. On the other side of the street is a small warehouse covered in rusted panels. Preston drove closer to the warehouse and spotted a white van on the left side. Preston noticed a group of guys standing by the van, wearing all black with their faces barely covered, stacking what appears to be bags of marijuana and cocaine in the back. Preston also noticed a black SUV beside the van with one man coming out, wearing a white suit with slick hair.

"There's the son of a bitch." Preston said as he sees Jonny Cartel.

Preston slowly put the car in park and turned off the vehicle. He exited out of the car and began walking toward the scene. As he walked closer, one of the men spotted him and started yelling. The other men looked up and see Preston. Jonny turned and stared at Preston. Preston does the same.

"Well, looks like the Instinct has found me." Jonny said. "What's the next step, Detective? I hope you're not here for a license plate or sticker check on my SUV here."

"I'm here to take your worthless self to prison. Unless you have another option of a location you'll like to take you?"

Jonny laughed as he looked toward his men. They laughed along with him, until Preston glared at them. Jonny turned back to Preston, looking at his clothes before keeping his attention focused on Preston.

"Look here, I got an hour before I leave for Miami. So, do me a favor, Maddox. Get a change in style of clothes for once. This whole intimidation approach isn't quite working for you when you're wearing only slacks and a casual jacket."

"I appreciate your generosity in the apparel department, Cartel. Though, I can care less on how you perceive someone's clothing. Anyway, that's not why I'm here and you know why I'm here standing before you and your pack of goons."

"OK, so what can I do to change your mind? Hmm? Give you some profit on the side? Hand you one of my nice fine women to keep you company for the time being?"

"I can care less about your greenbacks or your filthy whores you have stashed back at your place."

Preston held his ground quietly.

"I'm giving you a few choices to make. Either you can come with me, get in my car and I'll ship you off to prison or we can have ourselves a classic standoff where you and most of your men here are killed on the spot. Your decision, not mine."

Jonny stood quietly, not making a sound. Only staring at Preston. Preston kept his eyes locked on Cartel, not making any facial expressions of any kind.

"Tongue turned to lead, Cartel?"

Jonny walked toward the van. He tells his men to pack up

whatever they had in their hands and told them to leave the area. The men toss whatever they have into the van and they drive it off into the darkness of street. Preston and Jonny are the only two men at the warehouse.

"Alright, Maddox. Now you have a choice to make and make it right for yourself."

"OK. What are these choices you have in mind for myself that would make me accept them and leave you here to continue your pathetic way?'

Jonny moved his right hand to his side, revealing a revolver under the side of his jacket. Preston noticed it and looked up at Jonny.

"You sure you want to play this little round? I told you already. You want to go that route, you'll end up dead and possibly some of your men too."

"There is no other way around all of this. Now, you can choose your choice. Either you can go ahead and leave this area and don't make a second thought or I could just shoot you on the spot and leave your body to rot."

"So, if I choose the first one, I assume I'll live. If I take the second option, you're going to put one in me. Is that how this is going here?"

"You're smarter than how you dress yourself, Marshal."

"Funny. The decisions you've just gave me are similar to the choices that you gave to that woman I suppose."

Jonny stood frozen still, having what appeared to be a confused and worried look on his face. He shook his head before staying still.

"I'm afraid I don't know what you're talking about, Marshal."

"The woman, whose body was found in the river a few weeks ago. I know you're aware of the case. Only her torso was found floating in the water. Her lower body was discovered across town at some cannibal site where they were partially eating off of it. They eat mostly the thighs and some of the calves. Other than that, they still left some over for anyone to share."

"Holy shit Holy shit! God damn it! If you knew how she behaved and how she acted, you would know deep down that she deserved it, *Instinct!*."

"No, I don't know why. Probably will never figure out why you had her killed and fed to cannibals. But, overall, why did she deserve it? Is it because she didn't have enough federal reserve notes to pay her remaining price off?"

"She was nothing but a traitorous whore. Sneaking behind my back, working for that Ray Colby guy from Jersey since he just opened ship down here in my town. My town! That kind of shit doesn't play fair in my world of business, Maddox and you understand that don't you."

"I do. But, its none of my concern how you run your business. My concern is stopping your business and putting you in a cell or maybe six feet under."

Jonny started to shake, he held up the revolver, pointed at Preston. Preston stood still, starting at Cartel.

"You know what, I've just had enough of this! I have a plane to catch, Marshal. Big business meeting tomorrow. So, if you'll excuse me."

Jonny started walking toward the SUV. Preston stood his ground, with his right hand to his side. Jonny, still pointing the revolver, gets to the driver's seat of the SUV. Preston stared at Jonny with his hand still to his side. Jonny paused and shut the door as he started stomping toward Preston with the revolver.

"You take one step, you son of a bitch and I'm going to blow your fucking brains out all over this place, Instinct!"

"I wouldn't try that, Cartel. You wouldn't want to make a big mistake by killing a United States Marshal and ruining your world of business for a very long time to come. Even if you have a plane to catch for a supposed big business meeting. I'm sure your other clients and partners will understand what you've been through and will find a way for their business to continue in their eyes before they're caught on their own soil."

"I'll spell this out for you once and only this once. The only way I'll ever lose this business is OVER MY COLD, DECAYING, CORPSE!!!"

Preston pulled out his gun and fired shots toward Jonny in the chest a consecutive three times. Jonny slowly fell to the ground, dropping the revolver in the process. Preston walked toward Jonny, who's trying to reach for revolver while lying on the concrete pavement., Preston kicked it away from Jonny's hand. Jonny bled from his chest as his blood flowed around his body, soaking his suit.

"From the look of you on the ground holding your chest, you didn't listen to my warning, Cartel. I told you not to try anything like that."

"It doesn't matter, Marshal. Maybe I deserved to die. Maybe this is where my journey ends and all. But, soon, there will come a time where you are on the opposite end of a gunshot such as this and you'll be on the ground gasping for your breath. When the day comes that it happens, you'll know what's to come afterwards."

"I highly doubt your kind and strong prophetic words." Preston said with a smile. "But, whenever that day does arrive, I'll be in this same position and the other will be in the position that you're currently lying in."

Preston reached into his pocket, pulling out his black and silver Blackberry. He dialed 9-1-1. The phone started ringing and the 9-1-1 Operator is on the other end.

"9-1-1. Please state your immediate emergency."

"This is Preston Maddox. U.S. Marshal and secondary detective over at the New Haven Detective and Marshal Agency.

I've called because I'm currently standing around the West River, close to Orange Avenue at a warehouse. I need an ambulance and a coroner right away."

"An ambulance is on its way, Marshal. Should I assist backup as well?"

"No need for that ma'am. Just the ambulance and coroner will do just fine. I appreciate it and thank you."

He hung up and placed the smartphone back into his pocket. He walked over to Jonny. He kneeled in front of him as Cartel continued to gasp for his breath.

"Don't worry, Jonny. Ambulance is on its way. They'll do what they can for your sake."

"What about the coroner? Don't think I didn't hear that part."

"That's just in case you die here. Which is the most probability."

"Just go to hell, Marshal. Go to hell and burn for the rest of your eternal days."

Jonny's head cocked over as he exhaled his last breath. Jonny died on the spot as Preston only stared at his deceased body. He nodded and walked back to his car, leaving Jonny on the ground for the ambulance to find.

In a suburban neighborhood lies many homes of which families and friends live among each other. One of the homes has its lights on and inside of the home's kitchen is a forty-year old mother washing the dishes as her sixteen-year-old daughter sat in the living room in front of a fireplace watching the TV.

"What are you watching over there?"

"Just some random show. Nothing much on tonight, so I figured I would just watch something that grabbed my interest."

"Seems to me how you're pretty quiet over there that you're either in deep of the show or your bored by it."

"It's interesting so far, mom."

The daughter turned and looked toward the door. Hearing a tapping sound coming from outside. Noticing that the room is quiet except for the TV and her mother washing the dishes. She sat up from off the couch and walked slowly close to the door to see if the sound was coming from outside. The sound started again, this time alerting the mother. She looked over and turned to her daughter, who continued to approach the door.

"What was that outside?"

"I'm not sure. Sound like its right next to the door. Do you want me to go ahead and check it out?"

"Since you're already on your feet, I suggest you could. Just be cautious. There's no telling what that sound could be. Especially in a city like this."

The sound faded away as the daughter inched closer to the door. The mother continued washing the dishes as she glanced over toward her daughter and looked at what was playing on the TV. Hearing no sound, she looked at her daughter.

"Everything alright over there? You seem to be a little nervous?"

"I'm doing fine. Just taking precautions, that's all."

The daughter placed her hand on the doorknob and slowly turned the knob. Opening the door slightly, it gives a chilling creak as she opened the door. Upon seeing nothing or no one by the door, she releases a sigh of relief. The mother walked over toward the living room, seeing her daughter looking out the door and she went back to the kitchen.

"Haley, is everything alright? What are you doing?"

"I'm-"

As she responded to her mother, a hand covered by a black glove quickly reached in from the open creak on the left side of the door. The hand snatched Haley by her jaw and held her mouth shut. She tried to release a scream to gain her mother's attention. Hearing a series of bumping sounds coming from the front, the mother dried her hands and walked out of the kitchen.

"What in the hell are you doing in here?"

She stood in a frozen state as she saw Haley fighting off the black glove. Haley trued kicking out of the door at the individual's body, but the black glove held Haley tightly and slammed her head into the wall. Her mother stood covering her mouth with tears beginning to flow from her eyes.

"Oh my god. Haley, I'm coming."

As she took a step, another black glove reached out from behind her as it appeared the individual came through the back door nearby the kitchen. The intervals entered the home, their bodies appeared to be fit, wearing all black with their faces covered with solid black masks, to where even their eyes aren't revealed. The two individuals throw Haley and her mother against the walls and begin to pummel them to the floor. Both scream for help as they're being beaten.

<h1 style="text-align:center"><u>2</u></h1>

Officers arrived at a suburb home in the New Haven neighborhoods. They are heading through, going back and forth in and out of the home. An ambulance and coroner arrived on the scene as well. The paramedics entered the home with a stretcher, as do the coroner. A black car pulled up and out came Preston. He walked toward a fellow officer. The officer turned and was immediately what some would call star struck.

"U.S. Marshal and fellow New Haven detective, Preston Maddox." The Officer said. "It's an honor to meet you."

"It's an honor to meet you as well. So, what's the situation here, officer?"

"We received a call from one of the neighbors that something suspicious was occurring late last night at this house. From what we know, there were two females, one adult, the other, teenager. It seems that they were both murdered."

"Just being curious here, but, how were they murdered."

"I'll show you.' the Officer said. 'Follow me."

Preston followed the officer into the home. Inside, the home looked like your typical standard suburb home. A nice leather couch in the living room with a flat-screen TV, a beautiful kitchen with nice shiny tiles on the floor. The home currently filled and surrounded with officers, coroner, and forensic scientists. Preston looked inside the kitchen, to the left and seen the adult woman lying on the tile floor with her head severed.

Preston turned and said to the officer, "So, this is the mother. Couldn't really tell from a distance."

"Yes sir, the teenager is in the laundry room. Follow me, Marshal."

They walked into the laundry room, which is on the left side of the kitchen. Preston looked inside and noticed something red leaking from the dryer. He looked over to the officer and pointed to the dryer.

"Wait. Hold on a quick second. Please do not tell me that she's in there?" He asked.

"Marshal, I'm afraid she is." the officer said.

Another officer walked in and opened the dryer. The door widely opened as an arm flopped out, covered and dripping with blood. They looked inside and see that the teenage girl was shoved into the dryer and stayed inside while it was operating, in which tossed her around and killed her in the process. Preston and the officer left the laundry room, returned outside to their cars.

They walked out of the front door as Preston turned to the officer.

"What was the relationship between the adult and teenager?"

"They were mother and daughter. It was just them in the house at the time. The mother divorced a few months back and took the daughter with her."

"Should we contact the father of the daughter regarding this incident?"

The officer turned and looked toward Preston and said, "I think its best we do that after we get the bodies out of the house."

Preston walked toward his car, but the officer called him back, he walked over to him. The officer looked at little nervous, as if he's about to ask a unusual question.

"Marshal, I have a question to ask you." The officer said

enthusiastically.

"Go for it, officer"

"Why do they call you "*The Instinct*" exactly? I never understood the reason for it."

Preston smiled, rubbing his chin and turning his head, looking in another direction. He exhaled slowly before turning and looked at the officer with a mild smile.

"Look at it this way, everyone has instincts in their own sense of perception. It's what makes us do what we do. I just tend to use it all the time. If not most of the time. No hesitation in place of my career. I don't second guess, unless it's confuses the living hell out of me."

"I've always been curious of why you're called that. It must be cool to have a nickname in this line of work."

"Not exactly. From my perspective, nicknames today are now overrated. Don't have any sense of meaning to them."

"Really?" said a voice from behind Preston.

Preston turned and saw his boss, Eldon Ross, the chief commissioner of the New Haven Marshal and Detective Agency. Eldon is a man in his early fifties, wearing a button-down shirt with a nice tie and slacks. Eldon looked at Preston with a glare as he turned to the officer.

"You really believe what Preston's telling you, officer? Because if you are, that just makes you nothing but a rookie in this field."

"Well, sir, he's the Instinct." The officer said without hesitation. "I meant to say, yes sir."

"The Instinct. The only thing Preston could possibly be is a hard-headed guy who doesn't listen to the instructions he's given. Instead, he makes up his own schedule of work and does what he wants whenever he wants. Try convincing me that he's using his gut to make those decisions."

"Eldon, what have I done this time for you to arrive here

like this and call me out?"

"You know what you did. So, don't play those childlike games with me, Maddox. Your little incident from last night is quickly spreading around the entire agency and somewhat across the city. This isn't going to go well for you, me, or the agency."

"Eldon, let me explain the situation to you. A few weeks ago, I gave Cartel a choice to leave New Haven or he would meet us end by my hand. After those weeks had passed, I confronted him at one of his hiding spots, smuggling drugs. We talked for a bit as I gave him a short amount of time to leave and he made his decision right there. Besides, I've been on his trail for a few months now and it was getting tiresome."

Eldon shrugged his shoulders. "Yeah right. What else you have in terms of defense? Did you plan on talking him to death?"

"It was self-defense as well." Preston said. "He pulled first, and I fired the first shot. Which was the last shot before I called the police and coroner."

Eldon looked down and around the area as he rubbed his bald head. Glancing at the officers exiting the home. He looked at Preston. "Ok, once you're back at the office, we'll discuss all of this thoroughly and we'll find some way to get through your mess. alright."

"I'll see you back at the office, Eldon." Preston said as Eldon walked away from the area.

The officer walked over to Preston and said, "Jonny Cartel? The elite crime boss, Jonny Cartel."

"What about Cartel is getting you hyped up right now?"

"So, you really shot Jonny Cartel? You killed the bastard. How did it feel accomplishing it?"

Preston stared at the officer. He showed a faint smile before walking away.

"Something just had to be done about the man. That's all I can possibly say on the matter."

Preston walked to his car, gets inside and leaves the neighborhood, going to the Agency Office.

<u>**3**</u>

Preston arrived at the New Haven Marshal and Detective Agency. He walked into the front doors. Preston looked around and spotted everyone staring at him. Preston walked to the elevator and pressed the button. He stood waiting for the elevator door to open, so he can leave the lobby. One gentleman, wearing a grey suit walked by and looked at Preston. He does the same.

"Is there a problem, sir?" Preston said.

The gentleman turned his head and continued walking. Preston smiled as the elevator beeped and its door opened. He walked in and pressed the button for the third floor. The elevator door closed. He reached to the third floor and sees Eldon waiting for him in the head office. Preston walked toward the office as he passed by other detectives in their offices solving their own cases. Eldon sat behind his desk, surfing through the internet. He heard a knock on the door.

"Come on in, Preston."

Preston opened the door and walked in. "How did you know it was me that was walking through?"

"I can sense you from the elevator. Anyone can tell if you're in the building or not"

Preston smiled. "Funny. I'm sure you could. What did you need to talk to me about exactly?"

Eldon turned to Preston from the computer screen and

looked at him with a gaze. Preston glanced his eyes a bit across the office.

"The reason why you're here Preston is because of the actions you took by killing Jonny Cartel. You know what you did was a big mistake?"

"Are you sure it was a mistake. Because from my point of view, the man had to be stopped one way or another."

"Well, this agency doesn't go by your point of view, it goes by its Chief's point of view. Meaning me."

"I got that well enough."

"So, because of your actions. With a lot of thought and right timing as well. I've decided that you need someone to watch what you're doing on these cases."

"Wait a minute. Just hold on a second. What exactly do you mean someone will be looking out for me? Are you implying a suggestion that I might have a partner?"

"Yes, Preston. That's exactly what I'm suggesting. Look, this is how I see it. You shot Jonny Cartel out in the open with no hesitation. So, if you were to come across someone with a similar history, you would do the same to them. If not worse."

"Of course, that's the way I do my job. Besides, Eldon, I already told you that it was self-defense. Cartel pulled out his weapon first, he also threatened to kill me. So, what else was I supposed to do."

"You could've called backup you know."

"Call backup?" Preston said. "It wasn't that big of a deal. We were the only two there after he commanded his guys to leave."

Eldon leaned back in his chair, rocking in it to relax himself and feel comfortable. "So, overall, what's the big problem about having a partner?"

"My last partner worked on both sides of the law and to make it even crazier, the guy was a snitch."

"A snitch you say. Good thing your new partner only works on one side of the law. Our side of the law and I'll also add that she's very good at what she does anyway."

"Wait. She?" Preston said with a raised voice.

"Well, of course, Preston. Your new partner is a she. There's not a problem is there?"

Eldon looked at the door and waved his hand, signaled someone to come in. The individual walked in and stood by the door, just a few inches from where Preston sat. He hasn't looked behind him yet to see his new partner.

"Preston, here's your new partner. In the flesh I should say."

"Preston smirked. "Really. Let me get a good look at her."

Preston turned and sees his new partner. He looked at her from head to toe. She had nice straight blonde hair that reached near her shoulders and she wore a pair of blue jeans with a white buttoned-down shirt and a brown leather jacket to go with it. Preston smiled at her. She showed no emotion toward him, but only gave him a significant stare. As if she had no trust in him of any measure. Preston turned back to Eldon, smirking.

"This beautiful young woman is Emily Weston. A fellow United States Marshal and Detective from Newark in the state of New Jersey."

Preston turned again. "It's a pleasure to meet you, Ms. Weston."

"Same here." Emily said. "You look different than what I've heard."

"Do tell what you've heard about me. I'm sure the tales were pleasant enough to share to everyone, meaning me, myself, and I."

"Just that your what they call an angry man whose hell bent on claiming justice and changing the ways of civilization as we know it. Using your gun as the holy grail."

Preston laughed as Eldon chucked a bit. Emily stayed quiet with only a face with no emotion of any kind. Preston stopped laughing and noticed Emily's face. Eldon gave one more chuckle before glancing at Emily.

Emily is in her late twenties and her confidence gave her the shine of a woman who stood independent, able to get the job done. She looked toward Eldon.

"I've heard quite enough information about the murders that occurred in the neighborhood last night. I was only wondering how the investigation is currently operating?"

"The investigation is currently ongoing." said Eldon. "But, since you asked about it, you and Preston can go to the neighborhood and asks some of the neighbors about anything unusual that occurred that night."

"That's interesting enough to hear."

Preston looked at them both with a grin. Thinking to himself if he should give some words toward them. As the words near his tongue, he decides otherwise not to speak them.

"Um, pardon me, Eldon, I was planning on going over to a location where I know some answers could be currently available."

"That's Great. Even a better idea I could add to that. Since you brought it up and you apparently want some company, why don't you go ahead and take Emily with you on this."

"She can't go with me on this one." Preston said while smiling. "Besides, she's a well-established novice here in New Haven and no offense to her, but, I don't play well with others when it comes to the law and my tasks."

Emily turned to Preston and stared him in the eyes like a predator inching for a bite toward its prey.

"I could say the same about myself. In Newark, I did most of my work alone and had some help in some cases. So, look Preston, unlike some of the women that you've come across and met in your days, I'm not one of them. Nor do I fit in their caliber in any way, shape, or form. I'm just a woman that gets the job done whenever I can, however I can. With or without your assistance."

"Really?" Preston said. "You're saying you're some type of new breed of female detective. I'm sure I could dig up something from your past back in Jersey that could shake you up a bit."

"Not exactly. You'll hardly find anything on me that could lead to your gloating habits."

Emily turned to Eldon and asked for the address to the murder location. Eldon gave her the file of the location. She walked out of the office. Preston stood up and watched as Emily walked to the elevator. She turned to Eldon. Eldon is smirking at Preston.

"Listen, just try to work with her Preston." Eldon said. "Just try, please."

"Sure thing, I'll try. But, I won't like it." Preston said.

Preston left the office as Eldon goes back to the computer, still smiling about Preston's attitude toward Emily. Preston is outside as Emily waited for him at his car. Preston slowly walked towards the car. He sees Emily standing by the passenger's seat. He pointed at her and the car.

"Mind if I ask where's your car?"

"I thought I'll ride with you if you don't mind me." Emily said. "Don't want to waste gas on mine. You should be alright with that I presume."

Preston looked with a glint and said, "You have a nice valid point there."

Preston took out the keys and unlocked the car. Emily sits on the passenger's side as Preston sits into the driver's seat. He started the car and they left the office, driving to the neighborhood.

"Though, I hope you're standing next to the car when I

unlock it. So, that way I won't drive off without you and you can call on a cab to pick you up and drop you off."

As they drove down the streets, Emily turned and stared outside her window at all the locations around the area that they've passed by. Preston noticed and slightly turned toward her direction and watched her as she glanced the surrounding locations. Many vehicles are passing by as Preston entered onto the freeway. The number of passing and surrounding vehicles gives Emily a questioning though.

"Looking for something out there?" Preston asked. "You seem very on point looking at these places is all."

"No. I just never knew that New Haven was this crowded." Emily said. "Though it would be much smaller than what I'm currently seeing."

"We have our moments. Some days are good while the rest are bad. We get through it all. So, what brought you here to begin with?"

"Things became quiet around Newark, so I began looking for another location to work. Later, the agency began recruiting and some of the new detectives went to Newark and I was moved here."

"By the look on your face and the tone in your voice, you don't sound to happy about your transfer. Are you happy?"

"Honestly, I didn't expect to come here." Emily said. "I'm one of the best US Marshals in this country, so I believed they would send me to bigger places like New York, L.A., Miami, Las Vegas, Houston. Just somewhere big."

Preston smiled.

"Very soon, Ms. Weston, you'll realize that New Haven is bigger than it looks to be."

Emily looked. "Can't wait for that."

Currently at the New Haven Airport is Billy Bronson, a scruffy, scrawny, slim man who's wearing a flannel shirt with jeans and a denim jacket, also wearing a baseball cap. He walked towards the tunnel, seeing a lot of passengers walking in and out. He stood at the tunnel, scouted the area looking for someone. He caught someone from a distance and started straining his eyes to get a better look.

"Please let that be him." Billy said.

He finally sees the individual he's come to pick up. Billy walked over to him.

"There's my guy!"

The individual is known as Hoyt Bennett, a man in his late thirties, whose slim with bold features and hair that looked as if it's never been washed or combed. He's also wearing a long-sleeved buttoned shirt with jeans and black dress shoes. Hoyt walked over to Billy, smiling.

"Well, isn't it the great Billy Bronson. We meet once again in this crazy nonstop lifetime of ours."

"Hoyt Bennett. How long has it been, pal?"

They shook hands as Hoyt hugged Billy and patted him on the back. Billy decided to do the same. Hoyt picked up his bags as they walked through the airport.

"How have things been in New Haven since my little departure?"

"You know how this place works. The same old situation with the same old people. Sometimes, even new folks that comes across these ways."

"Billy, I'll say this. It's time to get things going since I'm back in town."

"How so? What do you have planned already?"

"In short words, Billy, it's time to blow some shit up."

Hoyt continued to smile as he started walking toward the exit doors of the airport Billy slowly followed him outside.

Shaking his head in uncertainly as to what's being planned in Hoyt's head.

NOIR
LOST IN SHADOWS
REMASTERED
TY'RON W. C. ROBINSON II

THE
PLEASURED
KILLING
AN INSTINCTS SHORT STORY
TY'RON W. C. ROBINSON II
NOIR

NOIR
AGENT
TREVOR
ONE MISSION
A SPY SHORT STORY

DARK TITAN
NOIR

COLLECTION

DECEMBER

ABOUT THE AUTHOR

Ty'Ron W. C. Robinson II is the author of several works of fiction. Including the *Dark Titan Universe Saga*, *The Haunted City Saga*, EverWar Universe, Symbolum Venatores, Frightened!, Instincts, and others. More information pertaining to the author and stories can be found at darktitanentertainment.com.

Twitter: @TyronRobinsonII

Twitter: @DarkTitan_
Instagram: @darktitanentertainment
Facebook: @DarkTitanEnt
Pinterest: @darktitanentertainment
YouTube: Dark Titan Entertainment